Quentin Blake

MRS ARMITAGE
Queen of the Road

A Tom Maschler Book
JONATHAN CAPE
LONDON

To careful drivers on both sides of the road

A JONATHAN CAPE BOOK: 0 224 06472 X

Published in Great Britain by Jonathan Cape,
an imprint of Random House Children's Books

This edition published 2003

1 3 5 7 9 10 8 6 4 2

Copyright © Quentin Blake, 2003

The right of Quentin Blake to be identified as
the author and illustrator of this work has been asserted
in accordance with the Copyright, Designs and Patents Act, 1988

RANDOM HOUSE CHILDREN'S BOOKS
61–63 Uxbridge Road, London W5 5SA
A division of The Random House Group Ltd
RANDOM HOUSE AUSTRALIA (PTY) LTD
20 Alfred Street, Milsons Point, Sydney,
New South Wales 2061, Australia
RANDOM HOUSE NEW ZEALAND LTD
18 Poland Road, Glenfield, Auckland 10, New Zealand
RANDOM HOUSE (PTY) LTD
Endulini, 5A Jubilee Road, Parktown 2193, South Africa

THE RANDOM HOUSE GROUP Limited Reg. No. 954009
www.kidsatrandomhouse.co.uk

A CIP catalogue record for this book is available from the British Library

Printed and bound in Singapore

One morning, Mrs Armitage came downstairs
and found a letter on the mat.

She read it to her faithful dog Breakspear. It said:

Dear Anastasia,

Because I am buying a new motorcycle, I shall
not need my old car any more. I would like
you to have it as a present. It is in the street outside.
Here are the keys.

       With love from,

          Your Uncle Cosmo

There was the car.

"It doesn't look very exciting, Breakspear,"
said Mrs Armitage. "But we'll give it a try."
They climbed into the car, and off they went.

They had not been going long when they
went over a big hole in the road:

bing   bong   dang   boing!

All the hubcaps fell off.

Mrs Armitage got out to look at the damage.
"Hubcaps," she said. "Who needs them?"
She took them off to the scrapheap, and
on they went.

But as they were going round the corner by
the vinegar works:

scrrunch.

The mudguard was ruined.

Mrs Armitage got out to look at the damage.
"Mudguards," she said. "Who needs them?"
She took them off to the scrapheap, and
on they went.

They were backing out of the scrapyard when:

skrrangg.

The front bumper had caught on an old bedstead.

Mrs Armitage got out to look at the damage.
"Bumpers," she said. "Who needs them?"
She threw the bumpers on to the scrapheap,
and drove away.

They were on their way past the supermarket when a lorry
backed into the street:

skerrunch

right into the bonnet.

Mrs Armitage got out to look at the damage.

"The bonnet," she said. "Who needs it?"

She took it off to the scrapheap, and on they went.

There was quite a traffic jam beside the new building site,
where a big crane was moving heavy blocks of concrete.
To and fro it went,
        to and fro,
           up and down,
               when suddenly –

kerrunch!

Mrs Armitage got out to look at the damage.
"A roof," she said. "Who needs it?"
She took it off to the scrapheap, and on they went.

"Breakspear," said Mrs Armitage, "I think it's time for us to get out of this town." They went down a side road into the country. All about them were trees, and the birds were singing.

"Breakspear," said Mrs Armitage,
"this is blissful."

But the road got bumpier and bumpier:

beding bedong bedang bedoing

klunk.

All the doors fell off, and the boot as well.

Mrs Armitage got out to look at the damage.

"All this stuff, Breakspear," she said, "who needs it?

Let's throw it all on the scrapheap, and be on our way."

But at that moment there was a roar.
It was Uncle Cosmo on his new bike.

His friends were there too – Gizzy and Lulu,
Ferdinando and Smudge.
They were out for a day's drive.

They all gathered round to look at Mrs Armitage's machine.

"Wow!" said Gizzy. "Wherever did you
get it? It's fantastic."

"We're off to the
Crazy Duck Café
for a game of
billiards and a can
of banana fizz,"
said Uncle Cosmo.

"You must come too!"

"But first, have
this leather
jacket," said
Smudge. "I've
grown too big
to wear it."

"And you must each have a collar," said Lulu.
"I don't need all three."

"And have one of our bendy masts," said Gizzy.
"We don't need both of them."

"And let me give you a motorhorn,"
said Ferdinando. "I don't need all five of them,
and it's always good to have a motorhorn."

Off they roared to the Crazy Duck Café.
And out in front, with her faithful dog Breakspear,
was Mrs Armitage,

Queen of the Road.